AF450288

Sorin Drăghici

This Sun which Blinds Me

NOVEL

Promovăm autorii români

CIP description of the National Library of Romania
Drăghici, SORIN
This Sun which Blinds Me / Sorin Drăghici
translated by Ana Maria Briana Belciug. - paperback.
- Otopeni: Letras, 2023
ISBN 978-630-312-347-9
821.135.1

Hardcover ISBN: 978-630-312-346-2
ePUB eBook ISBN: 978-630-312-353-0

Copyediting: Melissa Knight
Cover photo credits: Kanella Tragousti

Book distributed by www.piatadecarte.net, email:
office@piatadecarte.com.ro
Orders by phone. 021 367 5228 // 0787 708 844

For publication requests, you can contact the publishing house by
email: edituraletras@piatadecarte.com.ro
Letras Publishing House / www.letras.ro
contact@letras.ro

I

Greece for me, was beyond everything I had read or seen in the books my father gave me. Books which for years I could not put down. And now finally I was going there…

Eliza, my foster sister, despite being a silent girl, had said to me two days ago, `Maria, maybe this trip will bring you back from the imaginary and sick world you've buried yourself in.

What my sister had said to me that afternoon may sound strange, serious, and not exactly pleasant, but there was a dash of justice in her statement. I couldn't even think that what she had said was out of bad spirit. Not because I loved her unspeakably, but because exactly that `imaginary and sick` world that stood before her was my world. It was the most precious thing I had and it was like a sweet sin that only she, my sister, knew about. And, like every time something sweet is also a sin, the duality, the tearing I felt made me unsure: should I bury myself more in this world or come out of it? There were deep-rooted anguishes that would bear bittersweet fruit.

My father, a Greek teacher at the secondary school in Târgu Mureș, had tried successfully since I was 4 years old to use the Greek language when he talked to me. I grabbed everything that floated between us, father and daughter. For years, when he came home in the evening, with his tired forehead glistening in the light of the hall lamp, he would catch me as if in flight, pick me up and kiss me on the forehead, and then, until he sat down at the table where my mother served us dinner, he would not utter even a word in Romanian. He would ask me in Greek what I had done during the day, stroke my hair, open the folder in which he carried his books from home to school and show me what he had taught the children. He would ask me questions and then for my opinion on how he could bring his students closer to the language and culture he was teaching. He would tell me he would only like to have students like me, with my hunger for the Greek language and culture.

I never knew if he was telling me the truth or not, but either way our relationship allowed for many derailments from reality.

However, reality caught up with us, when my mother's stern voice was heard, halting our stories and forcing us to sit down at the table.

Often before we sat down at the table and immediately after we finished our discussions with my father, by necessity, we would exchange a complicit look with him, about my mother`s irritation for being out of our intellectual discussions. An irritation which would put an end to the stories.

This look was always immediately caught by my mother. She was unhappy with our complicity and the impenetrable wall created between me and him. She didn't speak Greek. Even though maternal feelings were constantly enveloping me in a safe and warm nest, I felt a slight coldness from my mother, like a breeze that I had perceived since childhood as one of sadness and disappointment.

„Ίσως είναι ένας ήρωας η τουλάχιστον ένας ημίθεος στο δρόμο σε αυτόν τον τόπο" – perhaps there is a hero or at least a halfgod in that country -, I had said, the day before leaving on what would turn out to be as an initiatory journey in my life. Dad thought I was alluding to one of the legends in the books I was devouring in the original language. He couldn't even imagine what was going through my head, an 18-year-old girl who had lived in a provincial town in Romania and who felt, with a certain sadness, the huge dissonance between the fantastic world of ancient Greece and the sometimes dry and boring reality.

Our status – me, Maria, enigmatic and aloof, and Eliza, a blonde and approachable angel – was already nailed down since middle school. My father, the deputy director of the school, and my mother, coming from the Molnár family, wealthy bourgeois for generations, offered us, apart from status, a home that emanated a wave of finesse and stability, beyond which nothing but admiration could result from the social equation. This was especially so because, 12 years ago, after everything that had followed at the end of the `political rehabilitation` of Great Romania, my father had decided to adopt a child from a family that had suffered a military massacre on Romania's border with Russia. The blond child, babbling only in Russian, had restored to my parents an emotional balance that they had lost almost instantly after I was born. Their marriage had been arranged years before the event, and was as a formality that served the morality, or the smooth running of family life with its deep valleys between slight hills of daily complacency. The Molnár family had seen in the gesture of the young parents a unique chance to restore the balance, disturbed by the exaggerated well-being of the family on a good moral line. The interwar Târgu Mureş talked a lot about the generous gesture of the young people who had adopted into the family a 'lost soul' from the edge of a country that had become surprisingly large after Trianon.

Mom was speechless when Dad brought the baby home—like a blond cake, wrapped in thick military-stamped blankets. But the times were steeped in patriarchal rules and rhythms, so fortunately my mother had to accept the fact that my father had brought a second child into the house. A child that no one had prepared her for, a child that she did not give birth to, a child that she did not nurse, a child that she did not even want. But the child remained. My mother, after recovering from the shock of not being the one to give new life to the family, grew to love this newcomer to the family more and more. I think she felt she could restore the balance of affection: even though she hadn't given birth to this child, she felt she still had a shot at bringing someone into her gravitational orbit. I belonged in this respect almost exclusively to my father.

Eliza had proved to be a child beyond all banality. She surprised more and more with an innate talent in singing, dancing, in quickly acquiring her new language and — always smiling — being liked by everyone. All that, without the slightest effort. Of course, for me, from the first resounding slap I applied to her not even five minutes after Dad brought her home, to the daily avalanche of praise showered on her by the whole family, everything was slowly turning into a growing heap of frustration.

By the time Eliza came into our lives, the whole universe had revolved around me. And because children in general often feel things that even adults can't explain, I felt that my mother was being tied to my sister, Eliza, by invisible strings that were getting stronger and stronger. Of course she paid a lot of attention to me too, but only my sister was that something that made her feel important again. She gave her wings. Dad, with his intellectual background and ambition to make his offspring a unique praline in a box of cheap sweets, turned to me almost daily. Our special world—just me and him—had remained untouched. Forever projected in a Greek `ille tempore` that only the two of us understood and felt.

`What do you want me to read, or do you prefer to talk about the myths of God ?` Tell me, my dear, what would you like me to read to you today? Or maybe you want to discuss Aesop's fables? `

My mother had always accepted our extravagance, mine and my father's, of which little by little she no longer understood anything. Neither linguistic nor symbolic. She only worried that my father was leading me by the hand down a path that was slowly but surely turning me into a rare bird that, to the rest of my family and schoolmates, was not of paradise but of perdition. From the beginning of the road opened by Aesop to the soon-to-be-poisoned antechamber of Socrates were strewn larger and larger philosopher's stones. Sometimes rocks, which I hit and bled. Sad. Ecstatic. Proud. Alone.

Despite my loneliness, I didn't really care what others thought of me. Perhaps not only because I had isolated myself in this solitary world in which I moved, but also because my interest in the outside world in the early years of my childhood was very limited. You see, father, you were the only one who came to me. You were the only one who entered "my house". You were the one I was waiting for to smile at me, to tell me stories, to protect me from real and imaginary dangers. I could never nestle on my mother's chest, safe from the cold world, like I nested on your chest. Even now, as a grown woman, I seek the pleasant, pungent smell of your body. That lived between the crocheted cotton loops of the sweater you wore, concentrated between your skin and the jacket you took to school every day; the olfactory essence of love.

I later tried to find this smell in my husband's clothes and skin, in the drawers and closets of your house after you were gone. However, this essence remained in my mind and was the definition of safety, of love for you. Could this scent ever disappear from my emotional arsenal? I hope that doesn't happen, because I don't know if I would have another point of support in the moments when there is no way out of the maze of cruel reality. I was afraid as a child, when family friends would come to our house and hug you or when my mother, in the rare moments of tenderness, would kiss you on the cheek in front of us, that someone would steal this scent from you. At night, before bed, when everything was speeding up under the rain of directives from mother, I would run in a moment of her inattention to your bedroom, search and quickly take one of your sweaters from the closet and bury my face in it for a few seconds, until some of your scent remained. I would run and hide under the duvet of my bed in the children's room. Eliza would lift herself up on one elbow to look at me, wondering every time where I've been and what the ritual is that I do for almost every night, before I go to bed.

I remember my mother often got angry when she discovered different objects that we collected under our beds. Branches with bizarre shapes and green with lichen, golden leaves collected from the yard and secret designs that no one should have discovered. Under this bed that served me, despite my mother's regular control, as a treasure box, I had once hidden a sweater of yours. It was a special sweater, a combination of wool and mohair that made it soft like a teddy bear. It had green and orange stripes and I used to muzzle it and roll up its sleeves so it became a fluffy ball that I could hide under the covers whenever I needed you. Whenever I felt like you needed to be somewhere other than near me: at school, with your friends, teachers, or with mom in the bedroom. You see, father, perhaps these thoughts would seem strange to you. Maybe this spell between us was too strong. Who could say whether it is so or otherwise... Formalities hardly ever had a place between us, father. But times were different than now, people showed their feelings differently, social conventions were much more important than love.

My classmates at school, if they met their parents on the street or at home, the first gesture they made was to kiss their parents' hands. I used to do this only with my mother. She sometimes changed this absolutely normal formality for her, as a gesture of grace, into an embrace. But I always felt, the moment I walked into the house, that this was the automatic gesture I was supposed to make towards my mother, and if she was having a good day, she would turn it into a hug. With you, however, things were different. When we entered the house, I would jump into your arms. My schoolmates they envied me for these gestures. Often, on the way home, I would break away from the group of friends because I had spotted you on the other sidewalk. We would hug like that, then

I would go back to my group of friends and you would continue on your way to the cafe or school.

Eliza had started to have a clear connection between rhythm and movement from an early age. My parents enrolled her in a ballet school run by Mrs. Tatiana, a graceful widow in black veils and always surrounded by a sea of little girls in white skirts. My sister was incredibly graceful with her angelic presence, her hair as long as wheat and her eyes as blue as the summer sky.

At the end of the six years at Mrs. Tatiana's, the ballet school organized a small festivity with `Swan Lake`, in a simplified version. My sister was like a magnolia flower fallen on a wave of a lake. The grace of the final melody, played by a violin, a cello and a piano (three members of the city's Philharmonic) seemed a perfect fit for her graceful, almost lascivious, but sure dance. A success. My parents hid in the hall, behind cheeks flushed with emotion, their pride for this pearl of the family. The little orphan was also the pride of the community of which I was a part: the social projection in meta-historical miniature of the Trianon success!

The whole room, kids and parents, were fascinated by my sister. Every family wanted such a model child. Eliza displayed a smile, often surprised, at every school or family success. She simply received laurells, she did not collect them. My parents had, of course, tried to somehow compensate for the inequality of the situation between the two children. Like now, in the small hall of the Philharmonic, where, after the festivities, they were trying to hug Eliza with their right hand and push me in front with their left hand, introducing me to the other parents. But without much success. No one was interested in me. Eliza wore the laurel wreath. I was just the standard girl: the overly smart, critical schoolchild who didn't help her classmates cheat during test time. Well, more than that: my performance - limited to school anyway - was disturbing. I often asked the teachers questions from the works of Herodotus, Epicurus, slowly, slowly alsoThales, which surprised them at first, but which annoyed them and made them see me, despite my school performance, as a thorn in a smooth and soft plain.

The only exception was Andonis, the young Greek teacher, who had slowly started to see me as a valuable partner, capable of taking him out of the instructive monotony. Meanwhile I saw him as something else.

Andonis married a Romanian woman, ten years ago. He came from Skopelos, an island belonging to the Sporadic Archipelago, and had arrived in Târgu Mureș after failed attempts to integrate socially and professionally in Bucharest. He was handsome, tall, with a thick beard. He spoke broken Romanian, which gave me almost exclusive communication with him at school. I was already attracted at the age of 11-12 by the gentle, distinguished and somewhat distant way in which he spoke to me. Although I had tried out of an instinct, which I couldn't explain at first, to get closer to him, Andonis kept a respectful distance from the model student. `Can I accompany you to the library?` I often asked him during long breaks. It was, of course, an excuse to be with him, only him, without the ignorant colleagues. He would turn me down elegantly and gently. Of course, I couldn't explain myself why he refused. I was sad that he wasn't giving me the attention I craved and wouldn't give me the opportunity to have a personal conversation with him. This frustrated me, even though I was just a kid, but it also motivated me to try again and again with other tricks.

Little by little, Adonis had turned into a forbidden fruit. My father, my only partner for long discussions in Greek, supplied me with all the books I devoured, and this enabled me to open and widen the avenue of free expression in this language, which had become my temple. It was the area where I moved naturally. The area that belonged only to me and where no one could steal anything from me. Dad had noticed for some time how in our discussions (in his office during evenings, always on Wednesdays and Saturdays) adjectives about the Greek teacher multiplied. If at first he ignored them and categorized them as harmless, a few months before our trip to Greece he had drawn my attention that everything that I, a 17-year-old girl, can expect from the Greek teacher, outside of the frames of education, is a chimera. He had done it carefully and decisively. I had to retreat another step deeper into my temple. However, if I think back, the discussions with him were in this strange interwar period, the only guide I had received from my parents regarding Eros.

My mother, a few years before, when I showed her terrified the crimson stain on the white sheet

I had slept on, she had told me that it was normal for a thirteen year old girl to start bleeding and not to have any dark thoughts. That's it. And although Eliza had gone through the inevitable phase of puberty more quickly, no one had revealed anything to me, nor my mother, or my sister.

We lived in a big, beautiful, old house with high ceilings and solid oak floors. It was one of the houses my mother's family had inherited from a wealthy relative. The house towered majestically on one of the small winding streets that sloped up towards the forested Plateau of the city, called Şomoş. Many houses on the street had a personality like that of a family member. The main entrance of our house had small bas-reliefs above the door, the chandeliers were large, like giant hands ready to caress our heads, the light filtered in through the forest that was beginning to thicken not far behind the house, the rooms emanated from every corner a faint, but pleasant smell, of long past times. Three times a day, the smell of whatever was cooking in the kitchen combined with those of the house and would envelop and embrace us in that something that I will always define as the notion of home. On balmy summer afternoons, when our big house regained its shady calm, we all retired to our `temples`. Mother embroidered endlessly in the living room and slowly filled all the walls with poetic tapestries, in which the boys wore flowered hats and the girls sat politely on some lake shore. Dad would retire to his study and work through the piles of books and papers that grew on the massive carved oak desk. Eliza was daydreaming about impossible pirouettes, lying on her bed in our bedroom. Andreea, housekeeper, governess and buffer in any critical situation of the family, made marmalade for the winter from the various aromatic fruits bought at the market and transferred them into 100 jars. The only quiet place where I could retreat for my rituals was Andreea's room. When we were younger, we often hid in her room, which overlooked the garden at the back of the house. It was relatively spacious, full of objects that made up the `Museum`. That's what my sister and I called it. Many times Mom or Dad would have to retrieve small silver figurines or mother-of-pearl inlaid boxes that we would steal from her room and store `safely` under the two beds in our bedroom.

This era had long passed, but I had rediscovered the potential of the room that saw Andreea only during the night. Since my Greek teacher had started to fill my fantasies, but to no avail, I discovered another talent, outside of the Greek language and culture: drawing. In the quiet nights, when my sister slept angelically in her bed, I imagined the world and life in ancient Greece: handsome men and graceful women who, scantily clad, paraded on marble slabs in the shade of columns or olive trees. They discussed the affairs of the `polis` or practiced their rhetoric on philosophical topics. These were images I associated with every aspect of antiquity, ever since my father had initiated me into this world past, but incredibly present to me. The illustrations that filled the books my father gave me had begun to give me a satisfaction, beyond the usual visual, a few months ago. I was fixated on a painting on a vessel from the classical period or on a mural fresco from archaeological settlements of the post-geometric period. The undulating bodies of strong, naked men, languidly embracing a graceful woman or an untamed bull, and sometimes another man, carried me into a hot and pleasant imaginary. I knew my father would not have liked me to linger longer on the painted pages than on those that carried the written ideas.

However, the imagination was taking its revenge and encouraging me. Stylized paintings were only the beginning, because soon they were not enough.

One Sunday, after we had returned from church and had lunch, my sister had packed a small bag and gone to the Philharmonic, where from the age of 15 she had assisted Tatiana in the preparation of the ballet performances that took place permanently in the beautiful Secession building of the Palace of Culture. I was alone in our room and, lying on the bed, I was leafing through an archeology treatise about the wonders discovered by a group of German archaeologists in Olympia, the cradle of the Olympic Games in Ancient Greece. The perfect image of Hermes, sculpted by Praxiteles, impressed me so much that I found a sheet of paper and a pencil and copied it through transparency. The perfection of the proportions and contours that I traced with the pencil, sliding from the beautiful shoulders to the thin but strong torso, to the perfect roundness of the buttocks, then smoothly descending to the thighs made me start to tremble all over. I closed my eyes and a wave of electrifying heat penetrated my every cell. The heavy breathing turned into a combination whimper and moan that I stifled in a millisecond of frightened lucidity into the pillow. I stayed with my eyes on the ceiling, confused for about half an hour. After that I hurriedly collected the paper and the pencil, the book and the drawing, for the rhythms of the house were beginning to be more lively. I could hear my father already in the living room talking to my mother. I didn't know what to do with the drawing. I finally tore it up into little, tiny pieces and threw it in the trash, after wrapping the pieces of paper in a dusting cloth.

The ritual had begun to be repeated relatively frequently. Whenever the family, in the languid rhythm of weekend afternoons retreated to the shadowy rooms of the house, I would take one of my thick books with magical images and find a refuge to meet my heroes, demigods or Greek gods.

Eliza was often at home, so I had made it a habit to enter Andrea's room without asking. Although my sister, a lovely, confident, slow-paced being, never took an interest in what I was doing or what I was reading, that Sunday afternoon she had looked for me in every nook and cranny of the house, without success. When, however, she burst into Andrea's room, she had found me lying on the bed with my flowery summer dress crumpled and stuffed between my thighs and with a drawing of a male nudity lying by the bed, obviously from

Ancient Greece, by the type of beard and strict sandals, with overly sexualized details in the pubic area. `What are you doing here, Maria, are you out of your mind?` Eliza had asked me, in a tone so frightened and confused, but so shrill, that my reverie had come to a very brutal end, in a second. The echo of her voice had run through the whole house, into my father's office, into my mother's tapestry, between the brass pans in Andrea's kitchen, and had frozen somewhere between our eyes, mine and Eliza's. The storm was not long in coming, for already rapid footsteps could be heard heading towards the back room of our huge house. `Where are you?`, dad's voice was coming closer and closer, `What happened?`, I could hear my mother, a little further back. Eliza tried at this moment to save me, as she never could.

All Elisa`s successes - in the family, on the stage, with friends, she magnetized them effortlessly.
I often felt the bitter taste that her countless flashes left on the roof of my mouth, but there was nothing to be done. However, she knew and felt that I loved her unconditionally, and animal jealousy had long remained in the history of our childhood.

Eliza had realized when our parents' footsteps could already be heard creaking on the wooden floors, that she had to do something. She gave me a little wake-up call and then bent down in a flash and with surprising presence of mind (she was generally slow and graceful) picked up the sheet of paper from the floor and quickly tore it into small pieces. Before I knew it and only seconds before the `Armada` arrived, she stuffed all the pieces of paper in her mouth and started chewing them and swallowing all the Greek porn and all my shame. By the time our parents had come through the door, she had moved to the window and mimed, muttering an interest directed beyond the window into the garden at the back of the house. `What are you doing here in Andrea's room? Haven't I told you many times that you are not allowed to enter here? What did you get off the shelves again?`, Dad said in a tone that betrayed severity, but also disappointment. `We wanted to see the back garden from above,` said my sister from the window. Meanwhile, I was already standing by the bed and had time, with the impetus my sister had given me, to formally arrange the bedspread and the flowery summer dress. My father, who knew our interest in Andrea's objects, said, `Come here to me at once and show me the pockets of the dresses.` While we were turning our pockets inside out, I realized how much intuition Eliza had, because if she hadn't swallowed the drawing, we would have immediately been confronted with a pseudo-archaeological reconstruction of a drawing that would have changed many things only for the worse.

＊

My dear Eliza! How much tenderness and kindness there was in everything you did or said about me. Whenever I felt in my childhood and then in my adult life that reality was overhellming me and there was no way out, I looked for you, found you and took you by the hand. Many things we did not say to each other neither in childhood nor after. It's like there was never sentimetality or drama between us. Your mere presence gave me security.

At the beginning of our childhood, there were hard times for me, when, willy-nilly, I always ended up in the `second row`. Your nature always gave you, without effort, a "soloist" position in all situations. At first this made me sick, because even though you came very early in our family, I still had the first-come reflex. I had the feeling, when we were very young, that you don't have the right to the same things that I had a natural right to. Our parents, luckily, tried and managed to keep a balance between the two of us. But the very fact that you were an angelic presence and there was absolutely no neccessity for you to fight for any rights, those rights clung to you effortlessly. Around the age of 10-11, I realized that there was firstly no chance, and secondly no sense to fight further for the right to sit in the `front row`. The forces that put you `first` were far stronger and far more enduring than anything I had strategically tried to set in motion in my childish head. The way you let me know that you didn't necessarily need the position that every situation gave you convinced me to let go of silly thoughts or revenge that only children can imagine. After this reflex relaxed in me, the years that followed in our childhood and adult life further confirmed to me that the most important thing in my adult life is you. The way you empowered me was almost invisible, the way you criticized me was always speechless. I have often imagined what it would be like to be as beautiful as you, what it would be like to dance as well as you, what it would be like to be loved by everyone as you were loved. But these games had at some point lost even their bitterness and were only games of my imagination.

After years and years of going through all kinds of beautiful and hard things, I even imagined what it would be like for me to have your husband and you to have mine. At this moment, however, all the doors of my imagination were closing, because my husband will be, in the moments when you will no longer be by my side, exactly the same strength that will stabilize me. How strange it is that the moment one sits in the `second row` of life, the perspective widens, the gaze shifts not only to the scene in front, but also to those who are in the "first row", but also to the right and to the left, behind and above, where key characters sometimes sit in the `lodge of life`. Perhaps the slight tendency to loneliness that I always had, and which seemed to many a misanthropy, developed precisely because of this position in the `second row`. But after I became an adult, I realized how comfortable the position was in the `second row armchair`, a soft red plush `armchair` that allowed me to be attentive, but sometimes inattentive, to lean forwards and watch the scene, but also lay back and snooze.

I know, dear Eliza, that though you loved me very much, you often thought me mad. Lunatic. Off to the plains with a sick imagination. However, you never gave me the impression that my quirks got in the way of your attachment to me. I remember that my mother was much stricter with me than with you. My mother always tried to pull me out of my imaginary world, but without success. Little misunderstandings in the family hung around my neck like heavy necklaces. She avoided comparing the two of us, but sometimes she got away with it and held you up as a model of behavior and grace. After a certain point, I was no longer interested or hurt by this. But there remained forever between me and my mother a feeling of me fighting for a title. I always imagined myself as a child that I had to prove things to my mother, that I had to show her that I was just as nice or non-demanding as you. Much, much later, when I had my children and you had none, I felt that this struggle was over in me. And that's when I understood what were the mistakes I shouldn't repeat with my children.

II

The trip to Greece, which my parents had been preparing for years, was symbolic for all of us. Dad had been to `Wonderland` four times before he married Mom. His family - the mother a washerwoman, and his father, an employee of the town hall hired to do inherent repairs in the dilapidated government building of the small town, not far from Târgu Mureș - had never had the chance to dream of such destinations or give their children the opportunity to see something else than the bottom of an dusty yard.

Dad had decided, after the first two years at the Faculty of Letters, department of ancient languages, to take a break and go to Greece for some time. His parents saw in his desire to go to Greece a breath of fresh air that allowed them to concentrate their decent financial reserves, at least for a while, in a direction other than that of his studies. He had left in a whirlwind with two friends and had only managed to freeze his college year thanks to a clumsily signed letter my grandfather had given him, in which it was written that the only way to keep Dad in college was to take a break for a year, so that the family can recover financially. After my father had arrived in Greece, he worked in the port of Piraeus for a month and in Hydra as a waiter's helper for several months. Every time he returned in the fall to resume his studies, he was seized with an unbridled longing for the Mediterranean sun left behind. He decided four times, with no idea when he would come back, to leave behind the gray and cold autumn of Bucharest and return to Greece. Thus, his student period had lasted almost 10 years. He had been an excellent student, but he was considered a `summer loser` in college and in his family, even though he wasn't. The summers were the ones he hadn't missed! They had given him, beyond the Greek he was studying at college, the vital `esprit` of the country he adored.

For my mother, this long-promised trip to Greece was exciting because she wanted to finally get in touch with this reality, essential to her husband, a reality that intrigued her enormously. Greece was in my mother's view like a virtual mistress of my father's, an immaterial but permanent presence. It was something that always stole her man. Even in their rare, intimate moments, she imagined her man flying with the thoughts to Greece, to a life in the sunny land. Greece had persisted and would continue to persist between them. He was fascinated, she was dazzled.

My mother had imagined in detail, before starting the trip, what clothes she would take with her, in such a way that she would be as elegant as possible, that there would be no competition between her and this virtual mistress. Months before departure, she tried to put herself in different imaginary poses, in different possible and impossible situations of this trip. She imagined how gracefully she would step from the vessel anchored on the quay, the look with which he intended to defy all the beautiful women who would cross her path. She was somewhat afraid that the clothes she had weren't up to par with those in European capitals, but she had a knack for putting small details on dresses or hats she'd inherited from her mother. In the months leading up to departure, the sewing machine took very few breaks. My mother was sewing and mending her dresses and our dresses at a frantic pace. Sometimes she stayed with the lamp on for half the night, and we could hear the rhythmic sound of the sewing machine pedal from our room. Dad hadn't given her many details about the road; he was keeping some secrets about the trip to surprise his family. Still, Mom envisioned herself walking gracefully through the streets of unfamiliar cities and on sunny beaches. She imagined this Greece as something very beautiful, but something that could jeopardize her and her family's stable future. She was projecting animal fears on this trip. She was afraid, without being able to put it into words, that she would lose my father and that she might lose Eliza too. I was already a lost cause from that point of view. For a very long time, Greece was the `Alpha and Omega` for me.

*

The journey was planned in several phases. We went by train to Bucharest, where we slept at a cousin of my mother. She was wealthy, like all of my mother's family, and lived alone in a house, or rather a villa, in the center of the city. On Victoria Boulevard, not far from the Royal Palace. A narrow bend opened into an inner courtyard, where the house's huge gate loomed with a glass fan set in a wrought-iron frame above the entrance. Nelly, mother's fickle and overweight cousin, was waiting for us at the top of the stairs. She was happy to see us. I didn't remember her. She had visited us more than ten years before. But what I remembered were the incredible sweets she sent us from time to time to Târgu Mureș. The same colorful fondants, delicious and filled with different creams, of hazelnut, pistachio and chocolate, sat in a pyramid on the table in the living room. We were exhausted, but all I could think about was fondant. I can`t recall what formal answers I gave to Nelly who wanted to know absolutely everything about us. Each piece of information related to the matriculation exam that we had passed magna cum laude, or our provincial life was punctuated with a fondant or a praline quickly thrown into our mouths. The moment my tongue touched the velvety surface of the praline and I felt its sweet aroma, all my taste buds were in a frenzy. The surfaces of the pralines were tough, and although my mouth filled with saliva, the sugary crust did not soften, but had to be broken with a slight pressure of the teeth. At that moment, fireworks opened in my mouth. I was in a sugary delirium. Off course we couldn't eat anything Nelly served us for dinner. All night I tossed and turned, without closing an eye, because of the pains and cramps caused by the immense amount of sweets I had consumed.

The next day, on the train to Thessaloniki, we each opened one of the four travel packages that Nelly had prepared for us. The surprise was huge: full of fondant. Not even a slice of bread. `Crime and Punishment`. Until we reached Thessaloniki I ate absolutely nothing. I drank only water and tea. When the train pulled into the station, I finally felt freed from the cage on the tracks that didn't seem to stop after the 40+ hour journey. My parents had looked at each other tenderly before getting off the train. It was as if Dad was introducing his real family background to his wife for the first time.

It was as if he was inviting her to enter his house. He protectively and proudly supported her down the steps of the train. Mother, blinded by the summer morning sun, smiled bewildered. But she was trying to live up to the symbolic moment and had slowly taken on the role of a princess on a formal visit to a prestigious royal court. Eliza and I were happy and giddy (I, like after a total fast), but the light and bustle of the station was magical.

We had to report to the small customs office in the train station. The officer could not stop his admiration that two members of this family from Romania spoke his language fluently. He had also called another colleague to marvel at this surprise and to serve us a Greek coffee, made in the kettle on the spot, in the corner of the office. It was the first coffee I drank until then. Dad discreetly motioned to me and Eliza that we could drink it. The aroma, which accompanied the almost instantaneous increase of the heart beat, catapulted us into another dimension. Everything, on the road between the mouth and the heart was an open gate, a fresh breeze, a little delirium that was not only gustatory, but also affective. A little bit of both. It was the first time that these two parts of our body communicated with this intensity. The same path, with ever-increasing intensity, would widen more and more in this country. We were going to discover eros. That something that connects on a vertical axis the mouth to the heart and then to the womb in still unsuspected vortices.

After Dad had cleared all our travel documents, he had been directed by the friendly officer with a list to the city's functional destinations: the hotel, where we would be staying for two nights, and the cruise desk at the port. In his kindness, the officer had ordered a car to take us all to the hotel he had recommended, without us having to deal with a taxi.

The two days in Thessaloniki were the preamble of this initiatory trip to Greece. The city was bustling with people. On the seafront, which was also the center of the city, stood a white tower. The symbol of Thessaloniki. It had been a prison, and now it served as a symbol. Axis of a cosmopolitan city, where you could hear, along with Greek, English, German, French, not infrequently Turkish or Hebrew. Everything was in motion. Everyone was talking loudly and cheerfully and had a body contact completely different from what I knew from Târgu Mureș. People hugged each other, kissed each other, sometimes three times on the cheek, held each other's arms, shook hands, and then held it with both hands for a few seconds, or patted each other amiably on the shoulder. Smiles flowed under the bright sun along the winding streets that inevitably led to this seafront promenade, which when it opened up to me — after a sharp turn in such a small street full of taverns — took my breath away! There was no water. It was a dark blue being that embraced the city with everything that bustled within it and shielded it from the burning sun. It seemed to dance with its waves to the rhythm of the people walking and talking on the beach. The picture was of unique perfection to me. `Father, is the sea so beautiful everywhere?` Eliza had asked. `My dear, `he said reverently, `the sea is different everywhere, every second. Not because it changes, but because each of us is different and changes every second. I know it in many places in Greece, but even though I know it's the same huge expanse of water, the sea is everywhere different for me too.` We were literally both sitting, even though we weren't really children anymore, with our mouths open on the cliff and listening to my father, who was already dressed in the role he dreamed of for years.

Dad insisted, after we settled in the modest hotel in the center, that we eat something traditional Greek on the terrace of a tavern. "Χωριάτικη" — peasant salad with tomatoes, cucumbers, onions, olives and feta — nice and cool. "Μουσακά" with eggplant, minced meat and cheese — filling and creamy. "Αρνάκι στο φωρυνο με πατάτες" - lamb with crispy potatoes, hearty and juicy — a taste explosion. The sensations were as if cut out of an unreal story. All our senses were stimulated and gently caressed. Maybe the tiredness, but mostly everything that unfolded before our eyes, made all four of us sit at the table on the terrace of the tavern like happy drug addicts, with a wide and cheerful smile. Dad was the only one who had retained a shred of rationality in those moments. Because he was the one who gave us the rhythm. After an hour and a half of gustatory bliss in the shade of the sycamore tree in front of the tavern, we set off — father in front, lanky in his gray traveling suit, with a white shirt, and we, the three graces, all in flowery summer skirts, wide-brimmed hats and low-heeled shoes — to a destination Dad already knew. `Τερκενλής` — an institution in Thessaloniki. We entered from the main promenade of the city through the huge glass door, into a pastry palace. Not only have I never seen anything like this in my life, but I never could have imagined (I was a `sweet tooth` and I always hunted sweets) that there could be so many varieties of cakes, cookies, pralines and chocolates in one place . All the shelves were tastefully decorated, but perhaps a little too opulent. A confectioner was showing off his skills in the middle of this huge room and was slowly decorating a kind of cake. The hot chocolate dripped in rising spirals on the body of the cake, which had already been covered with a layer of white chocolate. I could not tear my eyes away from what was happening in front of me. The sufferings related to the pralines in Bucharest were instantly erased from my brain. The confectioner who, I suspect, was used to daily customers uninterested in the show he was putting on, lascivious and slightly bored, had locked eyes with mine and had also remained suspended for two seconds with his gaze in the air, resulting in a small puddle of chocolate next to the cake. He had smiled at me and decided on the spot: the cake was no longer perfect for the display shelf, so he took it in his hand and, with a gesture that resembled a ritual sacrifice, cut it in two. `Please, miss, please, have a taste. It is «Τσουρέκι», a traditional specialty that we modify according to French pastry recipes`. I took the slice he handed me. I brought it to my lips, touched it and began to taste the chocolate glaze, the fluffy structure of aromatic cake, which, however, hid a surprise: a middle with chestnut cream. I felt at that moment that my lips and the roof of my mouth had lived in vain until then. The explosion of tastes, textures and aromas made me laugh so happily, but so voluptuously, that the confectioner could no longer explain himself the situation. To save the somewhat awkward moment, especially since my family had also returned to me after a short tour of the paradise shelves, I said `sir, the Φσουρέκι is like a kiss in the middle of summer`. He smiled contentedly, but Dad remained a little thoughtful.

A year later, when I told him that I wanted to marry the man who gave me my first kiss, he asked me how I already knew in Thessaloniki what a kiss in the middle of summer was like...

The wooden vessel, like a small city floating on the waves of the Aegean Sea, anchored after 15 hours of languid dancing in the harbour of Hydra. Dad accompanied us on the wooden deck of the vessel that connected once a week with Hydra, with Greek legends. Gods and demigods, heroes and goddesses, which he combined and recombined into miraculous stories, made my mother and Eliza's journey easy and funny. I was constantly irritated by the childishness of the stories. I was used to a different setting for these miraculous characters that formed my temple. I felt betrayed by my father, who had lowered himself to this level accessible to the "vulgar". Suddenly, all these gods and heroes that inhabited my mind, heart, and body were sitting down to play in the children's sandpit. `What happened to you, Maria? Why are you puffed up all the way? Don't you like travelling?` my mother asked me. `Yes,` I replied. `I'm a little dizzy from the waves. I think I'm seasick,` I continued. But I had actually realized at that moment, for the first time in my life, that the same reality means something completely different to each of us. Even if it's about your own family...

Hydra, the island that Dad considered his second home, was breathtakingly beautiful and wild. The port where our ship anchored was also `Chora`, the capital of the island. The houses, like cubes that climbed the slopes, went up and down smoothly towards the sea and were all painted white.
The churches were also white, but had blue or brick domes. In the afternoon sun, the domes seemed cut from the blue sky above them.

`Maria! It's incredible, it's wonderful, it's fabulous!`, Eliza had shouted. It was truly magical. I was speechless.

For my mother, the first image of Hydra was like a clear certainty of the fact that that something of father's, that `mistress` to which he was permanently attached, was of special beauty.

Dad had a lot of friends in Hydra. With some of them he corresponded frequently. Two sailors, who had fishing boats, and Giorgos, the owner of a shipping company, were waiting for us in the port. After the hugs that had lasted for what seemed like an eternity between dad and his friends, we had been introduced as well. All three men were aged between 40 and 45. They were handsome, olive-skinned, bearded, and full of smiles. It was Giorgos who, for four weeks, made available to us one of the houses he had in Chora. Our luggage was to accompany us on the backs of the donkeys, and we set off slowly, enchanted by the sunlight that was descending into the sea and the lights that were beginning to twinkle from the white houses, on labyrinthine, winding paths. We were heading towards the house that had been made available to us, on a hill. It was a cube with rounded edges, built on several levels. Each of us had a small room with a small terrace facing the harbor. The room accessories were simple, traditional, but very tasteful. The beds were made of mattresses placed on a rounded pedestal of stone painted white. The whiteness and external structure of the house extended endlessly into the interior forms of the rooms. It was as if the small town had swallowed us up in its simple and magical whiteness. I lit the candle sitting on a small table in front of the blue painted window and put a little sparkle in the sea of stars of the small town. I felt enveloped by an instant sensation of that `something` that my father always described.

I was home.

After the meal we had in the kitchen on the first level, we retired, each to his own room. I fell asleep. Dreamless. Like before a new start.

*

The next day, we went for a walk through the little winding streets of the town, to a destination beyond the crest of the hill, on which the white houses stretched. The destination was a neoclassical mansion: Giorgos's family home. His wife, together with his two sons, Andreas and Athanasios, were waiting for us at the gate. They were dressed festively, in light colors, with a lot of white. Athanasia, Giorgos's wife, was beautiful and distinguished, dyed blond. It seemed to be the flag of the family's steady situation. Slightly distant, but smiling. They were waiting for us with breakfast. Afterwards we were to take a tour of the island on one of Giorgos's boats. The garden in front of the house was a paradise: huge purple, white and pink bougainvillea trees, dwarf palms, figs, eucalyptus, olive trees.

Their house was huge, with very high ceilings and many nautical symbols. In the hall sat a handmade boat about 2 m long, made of a piece of wood that had been thrown by the sea on some beach, and of linen cloth. A miracle. `Who made this boat?` I asked instantly, in Greek. Athanasia and the two boys were speechless. `Μιλάς ελληνικα;` – `Do you speak Greek?` - they asked. I, with a tinge of naivety, which, however, hid pride, answered them: `Βεβαίως, είμαι μιος ελληνίδα` - `Of course, I'm half Greek`. Everyone started laughing out loud. But I had been very serious in what I had said. The sun, the sea, the small breaks with `μεζεδάκια – delicious morsels' injected us with a nectar that spread slowly, slowly in the cells of the body. My brown hair was losing its colour at the tips, turning blonde. Memories of continental Europe were fading and giving way to a floating in an undefined `now` of long, languid days.

We spent time with Giorgos' family, from the morning, when we had breakfast at their place, until the sunset, when the huge, white-painted boat brought us back to the port. My father would have long talks with Giorgos, and when he remembered that he had a family, he would turn to my mother and from time to time offer her a translation of what Athanasia had said. Domestic details that did not interest him and did not give him the satisfaction of a juicy translation. I didn't really get involved in their discussions either. I think my mother took it easy on me, knowing that I could translate for her, but she left me alone most of the time.

Eliza and I were enchanted by the two boys Athanasios and Andreas, from the first moment after we passed their doorstep. Athanasios was dark-haired, with slightly curly hair, a smooth, symmetrical face and a gentle smile. A rebellious streak danced in the wind on his high forehead. He had a beautiful body and was tall. Eliza followed him everywhere. With the rhythmic movements of her walk, with the waves of her blonde hair, with her white and transparent skin she was like a perfect antithesis in forming a metaphor with him. They didn't talk much, and I had to translate almost everything anyway, but they swam together, watched the sunset side by side, and exchanged glances while eating.

Andreas was older than the other three of us, who were 18 years old. He was 22 years old and a student in Athens, in his second year at the Faculty of Medicine. He was brown with a light complexion, towards blonde. He had a short beard and a wry smile. Those few years helping his father in the harbor had harmoniously defined the musculature of his entire body, so that every time he jumped into the water from the boat to swim, he looked like a statue come to life. In a kind of natural companionship, father was always around Giorgos, mother around Athanasia, Eliza around Athanasios, and me around Andreas. When he would catch wind and leap into the water from the prow of the boat and beckon me to follow him, I would remain suspended in time and space looking at an ancient statue flying towards the blue waves. „ Μα τι κάνεις Μαρία; έλα κι εσύ μέσα, γιατί είσαι πάντα κάπου αλλού;– What are you doing, Maria, do you come into the water too, why are you always thinking about something else?`

After a few moments, I would doze off, banish the ancient visions, and take a short getaway towards him and the blue sea.

On that particular afternoon we went around the island in the white boat and stopped near sea-washed rocks. The ship had anchored before lunch, which we had under a canvas stretched between two masts that kept us in the shade. The burning sun, the soft wind urged each of us to a little siesta in the languid rocking of the vessel. The rocks, about ten meters from the boat, were like slabs of limestone exposed to the sun. One wave at a time bathed their edges rhythmically. Andreas had jumped into the water and was calling me too. I followed him. We swam side by side, and after making a small detour to a rock that sat in the shade, protected from the sun, but also from visual contact with the vessel, we clambered over its edge. It was white and warm, smooth and inviting. We both lay on it, side by side, face up, looking at the blue sky that seemed like an infinite sea. He touched my hand. I remained motionless. He took my hand in his. My heart began to beat like a dove in the wind. After a few seconds, he turned to me and kissed my cheek. He lifted his head slightly from the white stone and looked at me with his blue eyes. I felt a warmth that enveloped me starting from my chest. He kissed me on the mouth. His lips were salty and soft, and his short beard caressed the thin, tender skin of my face. His firm tongue sought my tongue and enveloped it, beckoned it to a hidden dance between two bodies pressed against each other. The hug I gave him back opened a gate to a garden I didn't know, a wonderful garden that turned him, Andreas, into the eternal gardener. He was strong. His skin was smooth and covered a firm body with unsuspected ripples. He was the Hermes of Praxiteles. No!

It was my Hermes! He carried me tenderly in a maze of rounds, smiles, sweet-salty kisses, tight hugs and a taste of the sea. The heat that washed over me was for the first time one that didn't come from me. His warmth enveloped me and then seeped into the furthest recesses of my body and soul. He took me with him. Now I was him and he was me...

The rising tide began to caress our bowed legs at the edge of the limestone bed on which we had fallen asleep in each other's arms. We stood up startled, then we both burst out laughing. We jumped into the water to return to the boat. I turned my head towards that wonderful place. It was no longer in the shadows. The sun bathed it. A wave surged higher up the cliff and washed away a small red thread of blood.

III

Andreas and Athanasios both came, at the urging of their father - of socialist formation — to Bucharest in the 1940s, to escape the iron claws of the unstable and perverse political system in Greece. The government cooperated with the Greek royal house in a repressive and protectionist way.

The student group that Andreas had joined was not approved by the current government and caused him and the whole family a lot of trouble. The demonstrations organised by the students, starting from the courtyard of the Polytechnic Faculty of Athens, were intended to change the social and political situation in Greece. But the population was tired, the people were impoverished, and contented themselves with a permanent survival from day to day, where ideas were much less important than the daily struggle to be able to put something on the table. Andreas had been arrested several times, together with his colleagues, and the future did not look rosy. Although Giorgos, his father, had warned him several times to take it easy, he hadn't been able to change much. He came several times from Hydra to Athens, in attempts to calm Andreas down, but to no avail. Giorgos decided to send the two boys, despite Andreas's vehement protests, to Bucharest, after they had previously lived in Târgu Mureș for six months, in our house, where Dad dripped them like with a pipette 24 hours a day the Romanian language in their ears and on their tongues. I was my father's assistant, responsible for practicing the Romanian language in a more relaxed setting: bathing in Mureș, at dancing teas organized by Eliza's dance group, at walks on the Șomoș plateau that rose above the city. During the six months, Giorgos and Athanasia, the parents of the boys, had come twice to Târgu Mureș, because everything that had come together since our arrival in Hydra had almost inevitably led to two weddings!

I say almost inevitable because the cultural differences between our families, the ups and downs of the two languages, which were the bond between us, the immense distance between Hydra and Târgu Mureş meant nothing compared to the `sentimental storms of the beginning of the journey` that devastated our souls, despite the love that bound us.

"Dear Andreas!

I can't sleep now after watching the movie. I know you love me. I love you very much too, yet I am very, very afraid. I'm afraid for you, Andreas, lest you feel sorry for wanting to take me by your side and not the first one. Dear Andreas, please don't misunderstand me, because I know you love me, but I can never know if a day won't come - like in the movie we saw, when the boy's first love is looking for him and she finds him, after years and years...

I would like you to be happy, because then I will be too, but believe me I will feel it if you are not! I'm not jealous of your past and I tell you very frankly that I don't even care (at least not to the point where I start looking and asking), but because I already know you well and know that you can truly and sincerely love, I'm afraid that maybe (though it's not certain) after many, many years you'll realize that every man is capable of loving deeply only once in his life.

Oh, Lord, I wish we were not mistaken!

Maria"

"Dear Maria!

I am writing to you now, at night, a few hours after leaving, because I feel I must write to you.

Tuesday evening, after I came from Sighisoara, I didn't come to your place again, although it wasn't nice that, after buying the special gift for your father, I didn't congratulate him on his birthday. But you see, little Maria, I felt that you were not in your mood, that you were indisposed, and I did not come to you.

I got used to not listening to reason and rules of politeness, but only to instinct (like a wolf).

Today, before leaving for Bucharest, when I visited you, I really wanted to kiss you, but again my instinct made me give up. I gave up thinking about what you said to me on Sunday night. And then, on leaving, I kissed you, and you lowered your head and said to me "I don't want you to kiss me, but when I want to, I'll tell you". I respected your wish. You see, Maria, this is exactly what made me leave today without even touching you. It's terribly hard for me, but I do it because I love you and I love you more than I love myself. This made me write to you. I don't want you to excuse me for what I do, but I want you to understand me. Please forgive me if I upset you with what I wrote, but I only wrote the truth.

I fondly kiss you (only on paper),

Andreas

P.S.: I think you understand why I didn't want you to come to the train station."

*

It was a "double" wedding — Eliza's with Athanasios and mine with Andreas. We had 400 guests. Dad rented a mansion in Sângeorgiu de Mureş, where we partied two days continuously. Giorgos and Athanasia gave the wedding a Mediterranean spirit, with all the culinary details that the four chefs put into action. Athanasia spent five days with my mother behind the chefs, to give them all the necessary information to transform the traditional Transylvanian kitchen into a continental-mediterranean culinary fusion. Their experiment was a complete success, even if on the wedding day you could see an uncertain expression on the faces of the guests when they brought a completely unknown morsel to their mouths with a fork.

The whole wedding was a large-scale event, because our parents' guests came from near Târgu Mureş but the family's guests from Greece had to travel a long distance. Most of them came from Athens or Thessaloniki. Our house had to be almost completely restructured. Andrea's room, so symbolic to me, was turned into a guest room for the boys' parents. All the other guests from Greece, as well as the two boys, lived for a week in the mansion on the outskirts of the city, where the wedding took place afterwards.

Our parents and the boys' parents were beaming with happiness. Two families were coming together and building together a future that seemed like a dream. However, no one suspected that some dreams can turn, almost unconsciously, into nightmares.

I could never forget the autumn and winter of '44, in Bucharest because it was perhaps the most turbulent and difficult period of my life. It was all a hand-to-hand fight with the immediate existence of an uncertain and dark present.

At the end of the war, Andreas had entered, after continuing the Faculty of Medicine in Bucharest, a secondary school of internal medicine at the Colțea Hospital. His stable yet gentle personality always made him everyone's favorite, which continued at the hospital. Together with the professor of the cardiology department, he mainly dealt with children. Every day when he returned to the huge house that aunt Nelly left me as an inheritance, on Calea Victoriei, he told me in luxurious detail everything that had impressed him: the diagnoses that I did not understand and the borderline situations with which he faced and which impressed him to the point of tears. He was the man I had dreamed of, fallen in love with and loved unconditionally. "Maria, are you listening to me when I tell you what happened at the hospital or are you dreaming?", he often asked me, two to three minutes after finishing the daily story of the medical avatars. I heard him, but I didn't always listen to him, because I was fascinated by his whole being, the situation made me see him often surrounded by a pearly cloud, a kind of aura that hypnotized me. So I was stuck in a parallel reality, with my gaze fixed on that something that surrounded him at a distance of five to ten centimeters from his body.

"Tell me something about what happened at school, because also you have to deal with children, like me," he said. Then I would get lost in my reverie, gather my strength and short daily memories, and serve them to him, more willingly, more out of necessity, because I wasn't very talkative. I was talking more from the looks. Like at school, when my students from the high school would ask me something in the ancient Greek lesson - I was nothing but a teacher of classical languages - and I would stare at them for a few seconds, until one of the students found the answer to a question asked by another colleague. They had also gotten used to understanding me for a year, not only verbally, but also visually. Just like my family, where I was some kind of socially inexplicable phenomenon with my own rules and unpredictable functioning. But it was precisely this unpredictability that had brought me small satisfactions that went beyond what I thought ordinary days were or could be. The small Greek-speaking community had a cenacle that met in a small dead end, beyond Cişmigiu park, once a week. Andreas took me there in '42, to an evening dedicated to the wonderful Kavafis. The Genius of Modern Hellenism in Greek Literature. Hearing the members of the cenacle how stumbling and with what naive readiness they recited their pseudo-lyrical creations week after week, when Andreas took me with him, I decided to take up the pen!

„*O Rinokeros*

Έπρεπε να ρωτήσω τον ξάδερφό μου, τον ρινόκερο, πως διαχειρίζεται τα συναισθήματά του. Σε τι προβαίνει όταν βρίσκεται σε κατάσταση οργής, είναι ερωτευμένος, νιώθει μίσος και νιώθει άλλα έντονα συναισθήματα. Πως εξωτερικεύει τα συναισθήματά του και πως τα διοχετεύει μέσα από τους πόρους του δέρματός του.

Έπρεπε να το μάθω από μία καθαρή ανάγκη: είμαι άστεγος τώρα... είμαι ένας γυμνοσάλιαγκας παρότι έχω ένα κέλυφος-σπίτι στην πόλη και στη θάλασσα. Αλλά δεν έχω τίποτα να σκεπάζει την πλάτη μου για προστασία τη νύχτα.

Έτσι μου είπε ο ρινόκερος, θα έπρεπε να προβώ σε ενα τροπο για να σκληράνω το δέρμα μου. Συμφωνα με τον τροπο αυτο θα επρεπε να αλληθοριζω κοιταζοντας για ωρες στις κεραιες μου εως το δερμα μου μετατραπεί σε μια προστατευτική ασπίδα πάνω μου.

Έκανα αυτό που μου είπε. Όμως βρεθηκα σε ενα αδιέξοδο! Άρχισα να βλέπω διπλά καθως αλληθώριζα προς τις δυο μου κεραιες! Αλλά δεν ενιωθα να σκληραίνει η πέτσα μου. Δεν υπήρχε κανένα σημάδι καλύτερης προστασίας ή σθένους.

Υπήρχαν μόνο μία ζάλη, εμετός και δάκρυα...

Δεν μπορείς να βασιστείς στην οικογένεια σου...

Θέλω να γυρίσω στο σπίτι μου! Τώρα!"

"The Rhino

I had to ask my cousin the rhinoceros how he deals with feelings. What does he do when he gets nervous, when he falls in love, when he hates or when some emotion cracks him up. How they sneak their stuff from the inside out and the outside in through the pores of the skin.

I had to do this out of sheer necessity: I no longer have a home. I am a soft snail who has remained naked, although he has a home in the city and another at the lake. But I have nothing on my back to protect me at night.

He, the rhino, told me to do something to strengthen my skin. He told me to look hard and long at my horn and then it would grow a protective shield on me.

I did as you told me, Monsieur, but I came to a dilemma. I began to see double, because I looked hard and long at the two horns I have. I don't see any sign of my skin getting firmer, no sign of protection or strength. It was nothing but dizziness, vomiting and tears. It's clear: you can't rely on family! I want to go back to my house. Right now!"

This unpredictable furtiveness has saved me many moments of meaningless chatter with more distant family members or uninteresting friends. "I have something to prepare for the cenacle," I said; I stood up gracefully and said goodbye. Andreas, voluble and talkative, had no problem continuing the duties of host and indulging in interminable discussions, often bathed in countless decanters of Murfatlar wine. He only said, without a hint of irony, slightly raising his left eyebrow: "Maria has one more pearl to put in her literary necklace today." And so it was. My writings were little pearls. At least for me.

However, the real pearls of life turned out to be the fruits of our love. The first fruit was Lucia, a blonde girl with blue eyes like Andreas's. Although she was born chubby and has remained a beautiful fluffy doll all her life, I gave birth to her gently. As if by chance, at home, with the help of Andreas and my mother, who after more than 15 years since she had succinctly informed me about what happens physiologically in the body of a young woman, was again semi-absent, but in the right place. She was helping her only biological daughter cross a biological threshold — birth.

The months that followed were not easy. Romania had been moving on slippery ground for a long time, from a political point of view. The disintegration of the official position of the country, the precarious state of the services, the more and more serious shortages of the simplest household goods were a growing danger. But when the bombings at the end of the war became almost daily, the panic spread beyond the family's domestic boundaries.

Dad had stayed on in Târgu Mureș. My mother was with us and she helped me a lot. She was enjoying what I think was some sort of revenge on me. She gave me, day by day, more and more attention and helped me with a kind of hunger. She could finally offer herself to me alone. To her biological daughter, the first child, without being afraid of that moral balance she felt obliged to maintain between me and Eliza. Without having to stick to a plan that would satisfy her or Dad a promise she probably made in her youth. However, Eliza was present almost every day in our house. Whenever she could, she would come to see us or have lunch with us after finishing rehearsals at the Athenaeum, where she was the principal ballerina of the ensemble, or after the classes she taught at the Palace.

The Royal Palace had a magnificent reception hall, where the Royal House balls were held a few years ago. The wooden floor was, according to Eliza, extraordinary. A `large lake ` that made you want to give your best in dancing. Here she was allowed to give lessons to a few young noble girls, atavism of a bygone world, still clinging to aesthetic pulses trampled for several years by the boots of regime change. Eliza, as always, was pragmatic and immensely successful. Both on stage (although the last shows at the Athenaeum had been repeatedly canceled due to the political situation), and in the artistic world of Bucharest.

Some time, several months before my birth, she had been involved in a small scandal that could have pulled the rug from under her feet, but she got out of the whole situation clean. At the initiative of the cultural attache of Germany in Bucharest, a group of musicians and dancers from the famous "Friedrichstadtpalast" in Berlin decided to try their luck and stage, somewhere behind the front that devoured even the culture in Berlin, a show at which they worked on a long time. Due to the fact that in the meantime Athanasios had become the interim Minister of Culture (almost non-existent in Bucharest), the cultural attaché of Germany first asked him if he had any idea where he could organize such a show in Bucharest. `What an stellar moment!` – they both thought when they started involving Eliza in creating five shows in Bucharest. They swept a few irregularities out of the way of the project, but after they also convinced the Minister of Propaganda (de facto Minister of Culture in '43), everything seemed to be fine. The show had been conceived and directed in an antebellum Berlin, where culture, freedom of expression and the definition of aesthetics were at a peak never seen anywhere else in the world. Neither in New York, nor in Paris or London were such large-scale productions made. On stage was a combination of extravagant theater with elements of can-can, ballet and acrobatics, all seasoned with a scenographic technique that will leave you speechless. A total of 100 people came from Berlin. The production was called `Madness in a Nutshell`. Of the five planned performances, only two took place. Both, staged at *Teatrul de Revistă*, which had no productions of its own for a year and a half.

At the end of the second show, the fever and effervescence of success could be felt. Everyone — the spectators, amazed and satisfied, the artists, happy and exhausted, Eliza — was all in a floating bubble, and for the moment it made them forget that there was war, that people were dying, that there was no electricity, that soap was only to be found on the black market. After the performance, Eliza and the troupe of artists from Berlin asked the revue theater contributors if it would be possible for them to stay together backstage, celebrate the incredible success and not go straight back to the hotel as public regulation requested during the war. They remained. But the spontaneous party degenerated slightly, so when at 2:00 in the morning the police stormed the backstage of the theater, they found about 200 people in a Dionysian celebration, totally anachronistic for the year 1943: naked bodies, some coiled and embraced in bunches on the props, opium on the table, plenty of alcohol and two naked boys playing one on the saxophone and the other on the cello, like two musical pages. All other performances were suspended, the artists from Berlin had to leave Bucharest within 24 hours, and the director of *Teatrul de Revistă* (who hadn't even tasted the party) was dismissed. It took Athanasios two days to use all the levers of his ministerial position to get Eliza out of pretrial detention and another four weeks to restore her to her original position as prima ballerina at the Athenaeum.

My body was under hormonal siege after the birth of Lucia. Nursing, caring for this sweet and helpless creature created a physiological buffer that protected me from the horrors of war. I was in a protected bunker of my body and motherly love. I was exiled in a parallel reality. Andreas also felt this and was happy. He didn't keep me so much up to date with all the things he was doing at the hospital or the news of the war. I was like a warm and peaceful sun, gravitated by a few stable planets: Lucia, Mum, Andreas, Eliza and Athanasios. Times were terrible, but life went on.

It flowed like a little thread of honey from a spoon: slow, steady, quiet.

A few days after the end of the war, Eliza came to lunch and signaled that she wanted privately to talk to me. Lunch had been, as always, a little poor, but good. Our mother had served it in the salon. It was summer. The light filtered through the curtains and seemed to announce something new. Something strange — although the spirits had calmed somewhat since I knew we were no longer officially at war. After eating a little vanilla sherbet that I had made the day before and collecting the cutlery, Andreas left for the hospital again to make the evening visit and I asked my mother to hold Lucia in her arms until I exchange two words with Eliza in the study. I went with her into the back room, slightly darker and cooler. I languidly plopped down in the armchair where I often nursed Lucia and looked at Eliza. She was strangely and unusually confused. She had gone to the window where there was a desk on which were some sheets, on which I was writing some Greek poems. She had arranged them formally, taken a small bronze bust of Socrates and placed it over the stack of papers, like a stamp that seemed to seal something. An end of a road.

`Maria, we have to leave Bucharest! Athanasios and I will have to get out of here!` I was still surprised, but somewhat inattentive. `The Antonescu government no longer exists. The situation is easily crystallized, and there are rumors that the Russians will put in office only communists or officials who had nothing to do with the former government. Political or technical experience no longer matters, from now on. Regardless of how involved the ministries were in the nonsense of the war, regardless of whether the ministers and officials in the ministries were Germanophiles or Russophiles, they are all on the blacklist.` I was still puzzled. I didn't understand everything, but I was becoming more attentive. `The blacklist means military tribunal or deportation to a labor camp. Although Athanasios had a formal position and everyone knows that he was neither on the sidelines nor on his sleeve with the Government's right-wing policy, he is in the same pot as the others. There is briefly the possibility of obtaining a diplomatic passport which ensures an exile in a distant land. Argentine. Not everyone can benefit from this pinhole exit. Only those who were not in key positions. Some on high barricades will have to fall demonstratively. But we have the possibility to leave. I don't want to end up in a labor camp. Not again, maybe in

Russia. Dad won't be able to save me one more time. He's too old.`

Eliza tried to wrap up anecdotally what she had to say. I suddenly remembered what I had forgotten for decades: she was an orphan from a former part of Romania, which was now in present-day Russia. My eyes filled with tears. I didn't know what to say. Fate separated us again. At that moment, for the first time in my life, I had the feeling that Eliza had been an angelic visitor to our family. A spirit that has come and has to leave again, having set a family in order.

`Please do not cry! Please understand me! Please help me tell Mom! I have to tell her today. The day after tomorrow we leave for Madrid and from there to an unknown port in Portugal, and then take a ship to Buenos Aires.`

*

The void that Eliza left was like a primordial wasteland of our family. Andreas, with his presence — calm, smiling, handsome, was that `something` that spiced up the present blandness. Our family had remained an amorphous `something` after Eliza's departure. Our mother stared blankly, our father still reeling from the shock of not having been able to see his child before leaving. If before all the problems of reality drowned him in Greek literature and philosophy, since the glaucoma he had been suffering from for several years had taken much of his field of vision, he could no longer read. My mother returned to Târgu Mureș after Lucia stopped waking up every three hours at night. Dad needed her. The days passed in a tortured ritual. I had, even though the war was over, less and less of everything. Fortunately, Andreas sometimes received gifts from the patients, gifts that were almost always food. Lucia was growing up, and this tortured rhythm was punctuated only by a poem or an essay that I wrote in Greek at night, before the next feeding or by Eliza's rare letters.

*

The carousel of the 1940s was in full swing. As if a mechanism that promised a smooth dance had broken down and the speed was increasing more and more and the situation was about to get out of control. I felt almost constantly on the verge of falling out of the carousel seat. I was clinging spastically to the `handles of life`: Andreas and the two children - Lucia and Lucian. Lucian was born in a cold February. At the end of '46 we were forced to leave the wonderful house we lived in on Calea Victoriei. The house that Aunt Nelly left us was too stately, baroque and large, to house a young family of expats. It was nationalized and transformed into the seat of the Territorial Reorganization Office of the People's Republic. We received a small two-room apartment, near Cişmigiu, not far from the dilapidation where my dear poetry cenacle stopped working for three years. We lived in an old, ugly, unrenovated building. Above the gate was marked in stone a date: 1885. It was the year my father was born. Every time I entered the gate, a small knot of cotton would go up in my throat, which would roll there on the spot, until the tears came. Tears that told me daily the passing of time. I had arrived, even though I still felt young, to perceive the balance of life: a part behind me (Târgu Mures, Greece, the burning sun, my children, Eliza, the war) and a part in front of me (nostalgia, uncertainties, the precariousness of everyday life). The arms of the scale were, perhaps for the first time in my life, at the same level. They were swinging like a windmill on a bare mountain in Greece. A mill that grinds time. Sometimes forward, sometimes backward.

For my parents, time was running out, but only in one direction. My mother told me more about how sad my father was in her weekly letters. Although she tried to take him out of the house for a walk or to the market, she only succeeded in triggering fits of rage in a man whose diminished vision,
his imminent blindness, had robbed him of all the anchors of life. He lived on the books that populated his memories. He was like a traveler in a world that had formed over decades, like a sediment in the valleys of the cerebral convolutions of his brain . My mother was also worried because he had started, little by little, to answer and ask questions almost exclusively in Greek. `Dear Maria, your father's situation has forced me for a

few weeks to look in the pile of books he has, and in which he has also become a tourist, two books that make me laugh out loud: `Learn Greek quickly and efficiently` and `Don't be afraid of Greek grammar`. Finally, life forces me to make a truce with this language that was like a mistress to your father and like a nanny to you!`

My dear Andreas laughed with tears when I read the letter. He was the one who made me feel that life is not a machine that must be put into operation all the time, but that life is something that hides between the lines. I was always fascinated by this "something else" that he brought with him from Greece. An intrinsic "savoir vivre". Unhurried, relaxed and happy, in a crazy world. He had a warm soul that lived in a body that I adored and clung to night after night after I put the kids to bed in the next room. His smooth skin on his strong shoulders, the blond curls that caressed my face when I kissed his lips hidden in his short beard, his chest that danced rhythmically after falling asleep in my clasped arms, his thighs, his back that formed two dimples above his buttocks like a `chagrain` of pleasure filled me with immense happiness. I loved him as I had loved him from the beginning. And he gave me the flowers of love night after night.

After Lucia - strong and playful, Lucian - quiet and beautiful, came Laura - in '48, a child angel, and Liviu - in '50, a devil's cub. They were like the lines of a poem in iambic rhythm. They were woven all in an embroidery that put together the fabric of my hard life in the late 40s into a stable texture.

Fortunately, Andreas had become head of department, after passing his exams and his salary (not something special in the post-war years) plus the almost daily small "attentions" from the patients, kept us afloat. This is how we could help father and mother, who in the meantime had sold half of the valuables in the house, so that they could support themselves financially. Father could no longer work as a teacher, not even as a meditator of the offspring of the new nomenclature, because, apart from the fact that he could no longer see anything, he almost always refused to express himself in anything other than Greek. After every meal served by my mother, he would cross from the parlor to his study, touching every Greek statuette head on the long shelf in the hall: Plato, Aristotle, Aesop, Heraclitus, Socrates, Pythagoras, Sophocles. He said something to them, often asked them about who knows what, and remained fixed in front of them, waiting for the answer, or listening to the answer that only he could hear, until my mother called him from the drawing room: "Να έρθω για να σε βοηθήσω; Shall I come and help you with something?".

But that was something he never wanted, so he was moving further, fumbling.

" Όχι, ευχαριστώ αγάπη μου. Τα καταφέρω. Θα πάω στο γραφείο να εργαστώ. No thanks, dear. I can handle. I'm going to the study to finish something."

He would sit at his desk and sit there for hours motionless, in his world, which had withdrawn its borders into memories. Until mother called him to the table again.

IV

The `Infamous Decade` was slowly withdrawing its tentacles from the life and the city of the Argentines. The new president, Juan Domingo Peron, although surrounded by the "shadows" of his past, promised something new with his presence. Like all others before him, he saw the past as a sum of unacceptable mistakes and the future as a bird with large wings, free and on its way to a clear sky. Populist metaphorical content that Argentines had become accustomed to. But the "something" that made them fall into the trap again was the fact that, despite the political controversy of Argentina's neutrality until the penultimate hour of the war, something had changed in the country. Argentina had been forced by the political context to implement an industrialization that would substitute the import of products (after the semi-embargo with the Axis states), which had brought tens of thousands of workers to Buenos Aires.

Peron was idolized by the working class, and the new national plan offered them, beyond the right to live somewhere on the outskirts of the city, a kind of passport to the social and cultural life of the metropolis. The metropolis was pulsing, feeding its children with life and feeding on their energy and exuberance. Buenos Aires was, in the late 40s, a delirious mix. It was no coincidence to see a typist at one table in a select restaurant, and a personality from the city's elite at the other table. Journalist Florencio Escardo wrote about these years:

`No Porteno will feel uncomfortable, because in Buenos Aires there is no criterion for exclusivity, neither where you are born, nor wealth, nor intellectual tradition. Everything is open to all and the one who has a republican spirit will be respected. This lived democracy is perhaps the greatest moral achievement of this city.`

`La Boca' was the area that gave Eliza a sense of lasting happiness in Buenos Aires. Every time she walked along the streets dotted with houses, painted in various bright colors, she felt like she was on a dance stage she hadn't set foot on for several years. `La Boca` extended into `Sal Telmo` — the paradise of Argentine tango. Here, if she walked enchanted during the day, with the warm sun beating down on her face, she was accompanied from every corner to the next street corner by the rhythms of the various tango clubs rehearsing for the evening program.

She longed to enter one of them and feel the rhythm permeate her body, but she was, in this first period since they had settled in Buenos Aires, still shy. Shy and with a feeling that the artists inside might think she's a tourist. She wasn't into dancing, not even into the Argentinian tango that she had enjoyed many times in Bucharest, but in everyday life, she still was.

The Spanish language still did not flow fluently from her lips, the social system of Argentina was something new, she did not meet her neighbors yet, she had not yet made real friends. So she still had a lot of details that made her feel like a tourist, even though they already had official residence in Buenos Aires. Several times she had managed to convince Athanasios to come to "El Caminito" in the evening to see an Argentine tango concert, followed by a `Milonga`.

But he was not a passionate dancing partner, and the evenings, though very pleasant, for Eliza passed away in contemplative passivity. She was like a child in front of a display case full of candy, to which she only had visual access. Eliza's days, although she was discovering the city with pleasure and walking miles up and down the San Telmo neighborhood with its colonial-style buildings on the seafront in "Puerto Medero", on the "Avenida de 9 Julio" or in the "Plaza de la Republica". were monotonous. She had not yet found any useful preoccupation since they had come from Bucharest. She was happy that they were able to escape the clutches of a system change that would have destroyed her and Athanasios, but she couldn't find her place and she also had terrible insomnia.

Almost every night she woke up with the same nightmare around three o'clock and couldn't, or wasn't able to, go back to sleep. The nightmare varied slightly in the details, but the leitmotif was the same: they were all at their parents' house, in Târgu Mureș, at lunch, around the table, and Maria got up sumptuously to tell all the family members, her face bathed in tears, how much she loved her sister, who died after a traumatic accident. It was about her, Eliza, who paradoxically was also at the table, alive, thank god. The whole family: the parents, Maria, Andreas, their children, Athanasios were dressed in mourning, only she, Eliza, was not. And no one seemed to object that she was with them at the table, although they were all mourning for her. Many times, Athanasios had to calm her in the middle of the night, hug her and assure her that the dream was not reality and that he loved her very much. However, she was never able to sleep again after the nightmare.

Athanasios was already able, two months after they had left Bucharest, to find, through an acquaintance of his father in Greece, a stable position as a diplomatic cultural assistant at the Greek Embassy. They had not tried anything else, especially related to Romania, because they were afraid that the communist system, which was consolidating more and more in Bucharest, could reach them with a claw. Athanasios said with conviction that it was the first time in many years that he felt at ease when he went to work. In Bucharest he had a very good position in the ministry, but he was a `Xenos`, a non-native. Here, however, he was surrounded by Greeks, with their rhythms undisturbed or interfered with by other Balkan rhythms, as in Bucharest. Argentina was something totally different from Greece, from the

Balkan countries, so the Greek Embassy was an island absolutely independent and sovereign from Argentina's rhythms. The "ghettoization" was perfect at work, it gave him a security and psychological comfort useful in this second "reimplantation" in another country. His colleagues at the embassy loved him and he often saw them, over a glass of wine or at a restaurant. Several times he had invited three or four colleagues and their wives to their homes, and this gave Eliza the opportunity to have some social activity. Although Greek remained for her a square boulder that didn't quite roll harmoniously, body language (she was only a professional dancer) helped her a lot. She was a gracious and interesting host, and she prepared their dinners in detail days in advance. She liked to cook little culinary creations that she first prepared in two portions, before dinner, for herself and Athanasios, to convince herself that the Balkan "mélange" was acceptable at a festive table in Buenos Aires.

The apartment, which they had received immediately after their status as political refugees was accepted, was incredible. It wasn't very big, but it was near the "Recoletta" cemetery — an area of the city with beautiful colonial-style buildings. It had a bedroom, a living room that opened into a dining room, a spacious kitchen, and a small office. The ceiling was high and tastefully decorated in decent bas-reliefs. The floors were made of walnut wood and creaked tenderly, like in the house of her parents' in Târgu Mureş. Many times, after painful nightmares, Eliza would close the bedroom door and she would go out into the hall at night, where she would pace up and down, only to hear the floors creak. That's how she felt at home, in Romania, in Târgu Mureş, safe, protected.

For that sunny May Sunday, they had invited four families from the Greek Embassy, friends of Athanasios, for dinner. Eliza had been preparing for days and decided to cook Greek specialties for them, because they always complained about how poor the Greek culinary spirit is on the way from Europe to some restaurant in Argentina. She had bought a few bottles of Santorini wine (dry for the gentlemen, liqueur for the ladies) and had set to work, this time without the usual culinary rehearsal, in her spacious kitchen. As she hummed well-known Argentinian rhythms, which she embellished with improvisations, she undulated her lithe hips, bent her torso, dramatically tossed one ingredient at a time into the pot, languidly licked her fingers smeared with the tasty sauces. She had decided to start with a "Σπανακοπιτα" in the form of a snail, with a simple salad of boiled cantaloupe and reduced with a lemon olive oil dressing.

For the main course, not knowing what the guests preferred, she had ventured to make pork knuckle with bay and cinnamon in red wine, accompanied by a risotto and "Κοκορας κρασατος" - pasta with rooster legs in red wine. She had learned from Athanasios's mother about 10 years ago to make "Παστα φλορα", a simple but delicious cake with fig marmalade and a lattice biscuit topping. The guests had arrived, almost one after the other, around 6:00 p.m. They had each brought something Greek: a marmalade, a wine, a traditional contraband yogurt, an Ouzo. The four pairs were very similar: the men, slightly overweight and in their 40s, were raised in rich families on the outskirts of Athens and had always everything. It seemed that the only challenge they had at hand, after two or three glasses of wine, was to criticize Argentina or make comparisons exclusively favorable to Greece, from the weather to the public transport. Boring and typical of the Greek diaspora around the globe, Eliza often thought. The wives of these cheerful typists were more heterogeneous: two had been well married, coming from the same social status, but slightly more open-minded than their partners, and the other two, intelligent women with a lot of humor, who allowed themselves to play the role of "sarcastic chorus" when criticism began, meant to glorify Eternal Greece.

They were Ioana and Thalia. They were each about 35 years of age, and although they had not yet had to lift a finger for the welfare of their family, they had the attitude of women who would like to work something that would bring them active social satisfaction, an attitude of women who they somewhat broke from `traditional Greek embroidery`.

They had praised Eliza for her qualities as a host, they had remained speechless when they heard the political vicissitudes that had forced them to leave Romania, and they were absolutely convinced that she was the missing link in the `Balkan trio` set up in Buenos Aires. For Eliza, although things were happening quickly, this evening a dull veil had broken that had separated her from society, from the city where she lived. She enjoyed the chance to meet Ioana and Thalia, but she had no idea tonight how many things would change in her life, in the company of these two interesting women.

Two days after the introductory dinner, the two Greek women invited her to discover the city together. Their idea was to tour the famous Recoletta Cemetery, near which Eliza lived and which they had not visited before. The idea seemed slightly morbid, but the girls had insisted, so after drinking a red wine on the run in her kitchen, they had set off at 12:00 in the middle of the day, in a burning sun, to posthumously visit the flower of Argentina's past. They were all three slightly chipped, but that gave them a charm and a security with which they walked, laughing out loud and stumbling here and there over the marble slabs of the cemetery, towards a friendship that would give Eliza wings. In the afternoon, the three of them had a frugal dinner on a terrace in the "Plaza de Mayo", symbolically waving their silk shawls in the direction of the "Casa Rosada", the presidential palace, and decided to call the embassy from the restaurant's landline phone and to announce to their husbands, giggling slyly, that they would be coming home very late that evening. Thalia had had the spontaneous idea that the three of them should go that Friday night to "Marabu", a cabaret, a famous Argentine tango club. Eliza's heart was filled with a sensation she had last felt perhaps 15 years ago: reality was not just a straight corridor with no exit, but several doors opening left and right. And now she could put her hand, absolutely spontaneously and safely, on any doorknob and open any door she wanted.

The `Marabu` club was in a basement and they had to go down some steep stairs in semi-darkness. They tripped over each other a few times, roaring dionysian until they reached the club's reception hall. The porter smiled understandingly, like a father seeing his own giddy daughters for the first time. After they left their accessories in the wardrobe, Thalia- bubbly, beautiful and always self-confident - darted to the club manager (she had told the girls that she knew him). In five minutes they were sitting at one of the tables in the first row. The evening of the three young women was like a pearl in Eliza's new life. Ioana – a bucolic grace, Thalia — around whom the air vibrates with energy and Eliza — a blond and graceful angel with blue eyes. They were a visual magnet for the arriving guests which slowly filled the hall. From the first rhythms of the orchestra debuting on a stage in Buenos Aires, Eliza felt the music enter her every pore, warm her to the tips of her fingers and fill her with immense joy. The languid rhythm that combined with the melancholic violin solo ("Vaca") was like a thread on which memories from Romania, from Greece, moments of her life so far were strung, like pearls strung one after another on a thin and fragile thread. She sometimes smiled absent-mindedly, the glass of red wine in her hand. Sometimes a tear slipped down her cheek. At other times she felt she would spontaneously rise and begin to dance by herself, as if in an ecstatic ritual. She had never before felt such an epic dimension of music. During the first intermission of the orchestra, she noticed at one point that Thalia and Ioana, who were seated at the table in front of her, had suddenly begun to stare in surprise and giggle, discreetly gesturing towards something approaching from behind Eliza. She understood that the girls' attention was focused on a person who would soon arrive at their table, but she found it interesting that she didn't know who it was for a few moments. For a second the thought that Athanasios had come too had crossed her mind, but the thought was gone as soon as the mysterious person arrived at the table. He was a young, handsome man with a high forehead, sensually arched lips, and a complexion that contrasted erotically with his slicked back black hair. Thalia and Ioana had stopped giggling and turned, as soon as the handsome man had arrived at the table, into two languid ladies, put on a sensual parade. This had caused Eliza to let out a little girlish giggle, and while she was trying to make sense of the whole scene and brush a few unruly blonde locks from her forehead, the man simply introduced himself, `Good evening, beautiful ladies. My name is Juan. Juan D'Arienzo.

And I can't help but invite you to a glass of red wine. I observe the grace with which you amuse yourself at the table in front of the orchestra, and as I am here tonight to see the first performance on stage of these talented young people, I must accept that your presence in the audience's field of vision has greatly increased the quality of this musical evening.`

Thalia and Ioana obviously knew who this elegant and beautiful person was, but Eliza realized, without knowing who Juan d'Arienzo was, that they did not know him directly. Unfortunately, she didn't have the opportunity to ask them details, so she let herself be surprised.

The man motioned to a waitress who was taking the order, and he sat down in the empty seat next to them, never losing sight of Eliza. She realized for the first time that she was the reason this man had come to their table. They had spent, in magical rhythms, the second part of the concert, all four of them, sometimes teasing each other playfully, sometimes falling into melancholic and melodic reveries, sometimes describing anecdotal events from each other's lives. All this time, the half-darkness of the hall had enabled Juan d' Arienzo to catch Eliza's eye several times, to support, and to augment his look with a tender little smile. Without any hint of frivolity or "machoism". Eliza blushed, but luckily nobody could see it in the dimmed light. Each time the feeling of warm magic washed over her.

The next day, Eliza, Thalia, and Ioana met again for coffee to discuss the surprising evening at `Marabu`. Only then did Eliza find out that this Juan d' Arienzo was one of the most, if not the most famous musician on the Argentine tango scene. He was the famous conductor of the orchestra that had laid the foundations of the `Golden Age` of tango in perhaps the most famous club in Buenos Aires: `Chantecler`. Off course the girls had enjoyed the experience of last night, because they had been surprisingly involved in a whirlwind created by this superstar and had attracted all the eyes of the audience in the second part of the evening. But they knew all the same that the reason why Juan d'Arienzo had come to their table was Eliza. Reason enough for the lame jokes that the three young women were now enjoying to the full. Eliza felt that Buenos Aires was finally `home`.

In the weeks that followed this evening, Eliza had met Thalia three times in a cafe. And only with her. Why? Juan d'Arienzo had obtained Thalia's phone number through the club manager at `Marabu` and had called her several times, hoping that she would give him information about Eliza. Or a phone number, at least. But Thalia, although eager to become an indirect part of an interesting love story, had told Juan that she could not give him any details without Eliza's consent. Eliza felt tempted and somewhat attracted by the magic of this mysterious and handsome Juan, but the last turbulent years of her life tipped the balance arm, perhaps foolishly, towards the rational plate. Thalia laughed out loud in the cafes where they used to meet at the reasons Eliza gave for not meeting Juan: the Spanish language, Athanasios, the hard life, etc. Thalia was like a witch in pink with a diamond needle in her hand, relishing one by one popping all the black balloons that Eliza was blowing up.

In the end, perhaps more to get rid of her words, she had agreed to Thalia giving her phone number to Juan, on one condition: that he only call before dinner, when Athanasios was at the embassy.

One day after Thalia's last `struggle` with Eliza, at 10:00 in the morning the phone rang in Eliza's house. Juan's deep, warm voice had made Eliza feel an electrifying heat that seeped from her chest to her fingertips. Her vocabulary was suddenly reduced to monosyllabic formalities. She knew she would meet with him. She knew she would love him. She knew life was changing. Now and here, in this strange moment, with the phone receiver to her ear.

Romania's political situation in the first years after the war was sad, uncertain, perhaps sometimes more oppressive than during the war. I had the feeling, since I no longer had time and energy for my poems, for everything that had winged my Greek soul, that life had fallen into a strange "corporeality". Not always unpleasant, but very strange. The space in the small apartment near Cişmigiu could hardly accommodate six bodies, six souls always on the move. I had the feeling that everything that happened in the house produced a Brownian motion as in a soup of the whole family, even if it was perhaps only a flake out of the pillow falling on the carpet. We were all bound, connected, bodily dependent on each other. The procurement of basic food not only did not improve, but even compared to the war years it got worse, and sometimes I had the feeling that without the small gifts that Andreas brought home, we could only put potatoes and bread on the table every day . Eggs, chickens, cheese, fresh fruit and vegetables had become contraband in post-war Bucharest. Gift-bringing patients now replaced pralines and fine drinks in hospitals with eggs, parsley and tomatoes. The sense of smell and taste had returned, for all social strata, to a rural base. Even if the situation was a struggle from day to day, I felt safe, somehow in my element, in this corporeality: the first two children always nearby, the other two – Laura, then Liviu – linked to me through breastfeeding, Andreas with his caresses, kisses and beautiful body. I perceived everything as a sunset that enveloped me daily in a golden light that dripped on our bodies and between our bodies, like honey. Ever since Eliza and Athanasios had left Romania, I had the feeling that I was living on an island, somewhere far away, in an unknown ocean. I was on the phone for a few short minutes with Eliza – maybe once a month – and a few longer minutes with my parents – once a week. I knew that the situation of Eliza in Buenos Aires and my parents in Târgu Mureș was stable, but I had the feeling that everything had happened 100 years ago and everyone else, in fact everyone, was on another planet, inaccessible.

"My dear Maria!

I miss you all so much, but especially you, that this feeling tears me up night after night. I wake up disheveled and scared like a beaten stray dog. I have the same nightmare that haunts me. It's a strange and unreal nightmare. I don't want to make you sad by telling it I just want to tell you that the thought of you always brings me back to reality. I love you. I love you all. I miss home. However, you should know that we are doing very well here in Buenos Aires. I always imagine seeing Lucia, Lucian, Laura and Liviu running down the narrow sidewalks of Recoletta where we live, playing happily in the afternoon sun. I can't wait for better times to come so we can see each other here. I am not convinced that we will be able to come to Romania soon. We are further on a list of traitors to the country. Athanasios told me that a former colleague of his at the embassy had access to the list through a National Security agent. I think this is my cyclic destiny: on the run, from one place to another. Your family has become my family. Your country has become my country. Now I'm in another country, but it's slowly giving me the feeling of home. I wonder when I will have to go to other realms from here again? When will the Universe send me to other lands? Good! No more philosophy! I wanted to tell you that from the sweet monotony of beautiful Buenos Aires I finally penetrated the social life of the city. Two girlfriends, whom I know from the Greek Embassy, took me up and I went to tango clubs a few times. I personally met Juan d' Arienzo - the hottest tango musician with a talented orchestra at "Chantecler". This is an incredible club, an institution in the city. It's a place where every spectator feels like a king. This Juan has been giving me sweet eyes for a few months now, but I don't give a damn. I like him a lot, but for now I'm letting him court me because he's opening unsuspected doors for me: three days ago I met his agent, who will pave the way for an interview with the dance company that belongs to this famous club. Maria! I feel like I'm spreading my wings again! Life is Beautiful!

I hug you and enclose the letter, some small gifts for the children. Take care of yourself! I'll call you next week with reverse charge.

With love, Eliza"

Eliza had always put the letter in a package containing colored stockings for the children, chocolates, candies, sometimes a printed coat for the children, ladies' stockings, a few packs of cigars for Andreas, and the indispensable two beautiful tin boxes with fashionable colored prints which contained very delicious instant soups. Maria was very happy with the news Eliza wrote in her letters and the children were always delighted with the sweets. They had made a ritual of it every time the package arrived. They only opened it on weekends. After lunch, on Sundays, the children attacked the sweets, Andreas smoked a cigar, and Maria read them the letter, or passages from it - if Eliza slipped in any spicy details.

V

Eliza was laying like a cat on the hotel bed, the afternoon sun bathing her beautiful naked body in rhythmic rays, sometimes filtered by a veiled curtain that fluttered gently in the breeze. She felt strong, beautiful and in love. Her life seemed like a perfect, golden sphere rolling lazily across a sunny meadow. The only scratch on the smooth surface of the sphere was the fact that today, for the first time in her life, she had cheated on Athanasios. But strangely, she didn't feel guilty. She loved Athanasios, as she had always loved him. He was for her the same pole of safety in life. For several months, however, her life had changed. She had taken flight on a road that seemed to be hers alone. A sensation she hadn't experienced in years. She was no longer "under the times", she was above time and these difficult times.

She had been dancing twice a week in the "Chantecler" club troupe for about a year and had a real chance of soon becoming a soloist in three shows they wanted to tour all over South America. Every time she had a show, Juan had a reserved table in front of the stage, and although he had seen the three shows countless times, he came every time, alone or in the company of friends. Flowers were never missing. After rehearsals, Fridays and Saturdays, Eliza was also in "Chantecler" when Juan and his orchestra turned the club into a place of devilish exuberance with their music. Just like him, on Wednesdays and Thursdays, she also had a reserved table near the stage and was always enchanted by the melancholic, fiery rhythms of Argentine tango. This drug had also entered her blood. She couldn't live without it and sometimes she wondered if it was Juan or the music that had caught her in its nets. In the club, at the table that was reserved for her, in all these months she had never come alone on Fridays or Saturdays, because she was afraid of what might happen to her if she gave herself completely to this "drug". Ioana and Thalia accompanied her almost always. They were glad that Eliza had made it possible for them to be in "Chantecler" so often. The three young women reveled in a sincere and cheerful friendship, with all the social possibilities of this incredible

Buenos Aires of the 50s. They danced, laughed, flirted, loved life.

Eliza's two friends constantly urged her to make the move towards Juan. The decisive step. But Eliza did not feel ready. She was still savoring the electrifying preamble where she had everything she wanted, no compromise, no regrets. She smiled at Juan, this beautiful and tender Juan, sometimes from the stage, sometimes from the group of friends at the table, when he, conducting the orchestra, would suddenly turn and give her a warm smile. But strangely, she didn't feel guilty. Athanasios accompanied her to Juan's concerts a few times. He had done it to do Eliza a favor and to get out of the house, like all the worldly people, at the weekend. He wasn't enthusiastic about the Argentine tango, because he didn't feel its rhythm and fire, but he was happy to offer Eliza protective company. She felt safe and loved. Athanasios, however, seemed not to notice the smiles Juan gave Eliza when he suddenly turned in the middle of a melancholic violin chord to the audience. In this audience, for more than a year there was only her, Eliza, for Juan.

*

Athanasios had informed her two weeks before that he would fly with a delegation from the Greek embassy for four days to Santiago de Chile. He had asked Eliza if she would like to come too, but except for Sunday, when the delegation was to spend a day off in Val Paraiso, the program was official and held in the embassy building in Santiago. Eliza had decided to stay in Buenos Aires. Besides, she had a performance Thursday in "Chantecler," for which the dance company could not so quickly find a replacement. On Friday, it was decided to offer Ioana and Thalia a royal breakfast with a Romanian character. She had made an omelet with ham, polenta with cheese and had prepared, after two failed attempts in the last few months, on Thursday, after Athanasios had left, `papanasi`. This time they turned out great. In the afternoon they strolled in a hot sun on the seafront and commented, cheerfully and slightly frivolously, on all the outfits of the ladies who were doing the same thing as them. Exhausted from the sun and from the torrential laughter, they ended up in a restaurant-bar in "La Boca" for the evening, where they had a lot of fun with a group of five young women who came from São Paolo for the weekend in Buenos Aires.

This week, on Friday, Eliza had been absent from "Chantecler." But the next day, Saturday, like a little girl who forgot to do her homework for school, she took her place alone at the table reserved for her, only eyes and ears, waiting for the orchestra to arrive on stage. When Juan entered the stage, he looked for her with thirsty eyes. When he saw her sitting at the table, he stormed off the stage, to the surprise of the audience, and kissed her on the mouth. Then, quickly, he took the stage again. The program began with a "Lamento" in suave rhythms. Eliza was paralyzed for several minutes. Not out of wonder or shame, but because of a feeling she didn't remember feeling with such intensity before: love.

She had her eyes fixed on Juan. The music could be heard very far away, almost imperceptible, and the audience and the hall no longer existed. She was happy. After the concert he asked her, with the fear of a frightened boy, why she had not been in the "Chantecler" on Friday. Eliza told him about the crazy day she had with the girls, and he calmly caressed her hair. For the first time, Eliza did not let him know by any elegant gesture she did not want his touch. Holding hands, tender, a little scared, their hearts pounding in their chests in unfamiliar rhythms, they walked towards Juan's apartment. Time seemed to dissolve. Their chained bodies finally wanted to quench the thirst they had felt for each other for so long. The love between them opened like an exotic flower, revealing in this night colors and scents that Eliza had thought did not exist.

The sunny morning found them hugging, with a smile on their faces. Juan hadn't asked her at all why matrimonial duties didn't call her home. He was happy and that was enough. When Eliza told him, towards noon, rising slowly from his embrace, that she would have to go, he had not protested. He had just raised his left eyebrow slightly and said "thank you". Eliza dressed with slow movements. The smile was still there on her lips, and it sent unseen extensions throughout her body.

Walking down the street in front of the house where Juan lived, she felt like she was enveloped in light. A lot of light. She had decided to cross to the tram station around the corner. She stepped off the pavement like in a dream, with a light step, and then, almost instantly, she felt a heavy thump. The light became unbearable for a second. Then suddenly everything went dark.

*

I had seen my parents for the last time two weeks ago, when I decided that during Andreas' vacation I would leave the four children with him in Bucharest for two days, and go see them in Târgu Mureș. A trip with the whole family would have been tiring and complicated, until Liviu was a little older.

I fell in love again with Târgu Mureș. It was so quiet here. The rhythms of the city were of a fair forgotten by time and, compared to the hectic and crowded Bucharest, I had the feeling that the air here is breathable and calm. My parents were like two figures in a picture hanging on the wall. They hadn't changed much. Mom was still functioning in good shape, Dad was shrouded in a milky halo of dementia that cut him off from everyone and everything most of the day. I had promised them that we would all see each other, again, in Bucharest, when Liviu was 3 years old.

Now, all gathered in our small and cramped house in Bucharest, we were going to open the package that we had received from Eliza, the very day I had left for Târgu Mureș.

This ritual always brought me and my family indescribable joy. Today we were going to enjoy the Argentinian goodies and read Eliza's letter, which was always carefully slipped into a green envelope among the gifts. And finally, since Eliza left Romania, all eight of us have been doing this, together, gathered around the Sunday table. I hadn't seen my parents so emotional, hugging each other with tears in their eyes, since decades.

The apartment near Cișmigiu had become microscopic, in the few days since my parents were visiting us. Every corner of the house had acquired a function. To sleep, to play, to snooze, to read. The three generations functioned as an organism radiating love. On Sunday, my mother and I had prepared a festive meal from the goodies we bought in Obor market and from the gifts received from the hospital . Me, without unpacking all the gifts from Buenos Aires, which I had received two weeks ago, had groped out of the package the well-known colored tin box containing Argentine instant soup. Every time I made a combination between this magic powder and the vegetables from Obor market. A miracle of soup came out every time. Although I had put in many choice ingredients:

carrots, celery, fresh parsley, the soup tasted quite strange. The steak and baked potatoes, the sauerkraut, the apple pie, however, turned out delicious. We were all gathered around the table. Happy, noisy, hungry people. We each ate only one or two spoonfuls of the soup (in the evening after dinner, my mother and I decided to flush it down the toilet - it was not what she had wanted either), but the steak disappeared from the table in a few minutes, like the apple cake, with its caramelized crust.

Eliza's package was full of gifts for everyone: two flowered spring dresses for Lucia and Laura, two tin cars for Lucian and Liviu, the indispensable cigars for Andreas, an album of black and white photographs of the Argentine tango nightlife that she had also sent to my parents, a cute little shoulder bag for me. There were still teddy bear chocolates at the bottom of the box, but I hadn't found the letter. For the first time there was no green envelope slipped between the presents. It felt strange, but I had thought that Eliza had probably forgotten to slip it in before putting the package in the post office. Anyway, we were going to talk on the phone in 10 days, as we had arranged a month ago.

✳

Two days after my parents had returned to Târgu Mureș, when the rhythms of the house had already returned to normal, I picked up a registered letter from the postman, around 10 in the morning. It was from Argentina. The senders were Eliza and Athanasios. But the envelope was white, not green, as usual. Very white and bright. Disturbingly white.

I sat down in the hall, on the chair next to the wardrobe, where a ray of sunlight entered from the kitchen window. I let the light flood my face for a few seconds, then opened the letter with quick and agitated gestures.

`Dear Maria, dear Andreas!*

This time I am writing to you, and not, as usual, Eliza. The package that Eliza prepared for you a long time ago, and which I will post as usual, but only in a week, does not contain her letter. Eliza used to write it the day before she put the package in the post.

But Eliza is no longer between us. It breaks my heart into a thousand pieces every time I think that I have to write this to you and not say it as we hug each other in tears.

She was hit by a tram on a Sunday afternoon while walking in Buenos Aires. She left us on the spot. She didn't suffer, the doctors told me. Before leaving Romania, Eliza and I promised each other that, whatever happens, we want to find our eternal rest in the family vault in Târgu Mureş. However, transporting her lifeless body from Argentina to Romania is beyond my financial means. I decided to cremate her. I will also come to Romania in eight weeks and there is a risk of being arrested. But I want us all to be together, to take her on her last journey. I cannot do the shipping of the ashes from Argentina, so I am sending you this letter in advance, one week before I send the package. I hope that the letter will not be checked by the customs officials, as our telephone conversations are tapped. I want you to receive this letter before you receive the package!

This time I left only one of the tin cans of instant soup in the package prepared by Eliza. But instead of soup dust, I put her ashes in the colored box. This is the easiest way for the ashes of her body to reach Romania. Please call me on the reverse charge phone as soon as you receive the letter.

I hold you sorrowfully, as I have never been before in this life. Be strong. We'll be together soon.

Athanasios"

Maria looked up, nothing on her mind, towards the ray of sunlight that faced her face. The light became unbearable for a second, then suddenly everything went dark.